For Moses Renee and Curtis Flood—B.P.

To my parents—J.A.

Text copyright © 2018 by Baptiste Paul.
Illustrations copyright © 2018 by Jacqueline Alcántara.
First published in the United States, Great Britain, Canada, Australia, and New Zealand in 2018
by NorthSouth Books, Inc., an imprint of NordSüd Verlag AG, CH-8050 Zürich, Switzerland.

Distributed in the United States by NorthSouth Books, Inc., New York 10016.
Library of Congress Cataloging-in-Publication Data is available.
ISBN: 978-0-7358-4312-7
Printed in the United States, 2018
3 5 7 9 · 10 8 6 4 2
www.northsouth.com

THE FIELD

words by **Baptiste Paul** · pictures by **Jacqueline Alcántara**

North
South

Vini! Come!
The field calls.

Bol. Ball.

Soulye. Shoes.

Goal. Goal.

Ou. Ou. Ou. You. You. You.
Friends versus friends.

Annou ale! Let's go!

Uh-oh.

Shutters bang.
Sun hides.
Clay dust stings.
Sky falls.

Fini? Game over?

Rain stops.
Sun peeks.

One last drive.
Dribble, twist...

GOOOOOOOOOOOOOOOOAL!

High fives.
Fist-bumps.
Happy tackles.

Mamas call.
Vini! Come!

We play on.

Vini, abwezan! Come now!

Game pauses.

Mamas press their lips.

Soaked shoes.
Dirty shirts.
Mud-caked kids.
Torn-up field.

We hide our smiles.
We slip into the tub.

Bonswè. Good night.

We dream about *futbol*.
We dream about friends.
Until the field calls again.

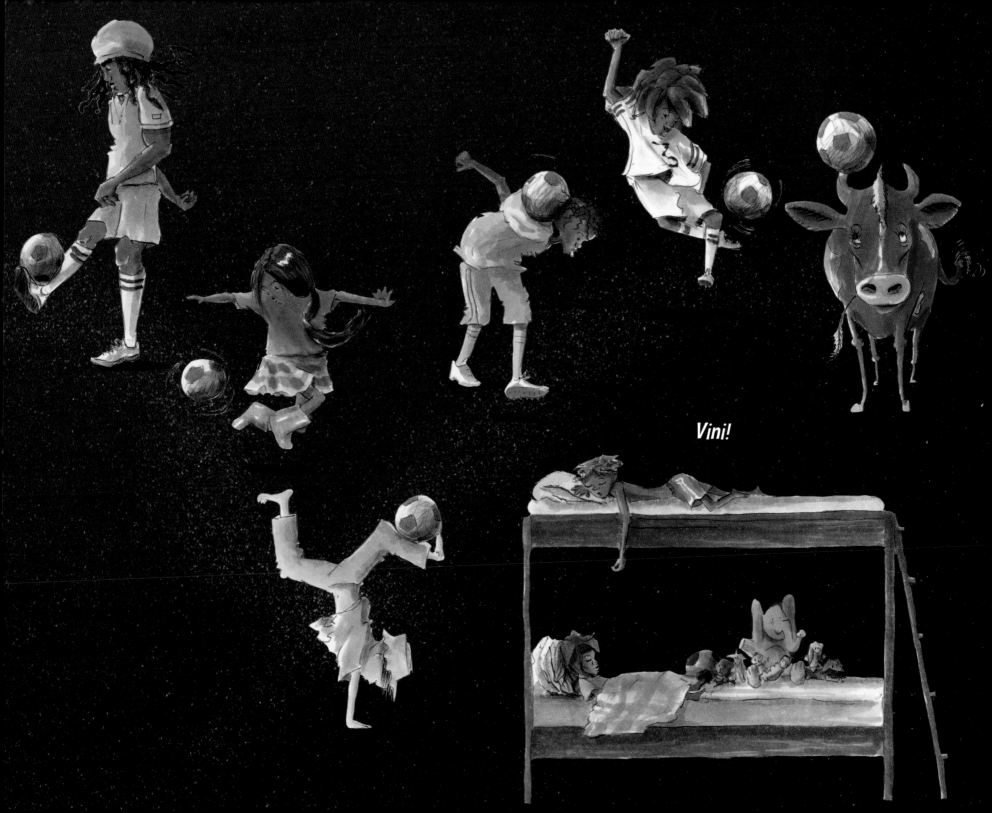

Vini!

Author's Note

As a kid growing up, I did not have electricity, running water, or many toys. What I did have plenty of were siblings—nine of them—and lots of friends. Most of my free time was spent on a *futbol* (soccer) field playing, learning new techniques, and occasionally getting bruised. When I see my children run outside to play, it reminds me of my childhood.

In *The Field*, children overcome many barriers that threaten to end their game. In life, things rarely happen as we plan, but the way we keep playing through challenges makes us who we are. Today, I still get the chills watching a soccer game. I go crazy or, what my son would say, "coo coo nuts" when my team scores a GOOOOOOOAAALLLL! I love the concept of play: everyone cheering together, forgetting about whatever challenges life can bring.

Creole is a language spoken by peoples of several Caribbean islands, including Haiti, Saint Lucia, and Dominica. In *The Field*, you'll notice that some of the Saint Lucian Creole words are similar to French, English, Hindi, and other languages—because many people who live on the island either speak or have ancestors who spoke these languages.

Even more amazing is that since people rarely write in Creole (they mostly speak it), new words are always being added and older words tend to change or get forgotten. This is one reason each island's "Creole" sounds a little different.

Bibliography (for Saint Lucian Creole spellings/accent marks)
Crosbie, Paul, et al. *Kwéyòl Dictionary*. Edited by David Frank, 1st ed., Castries, Saint Lucia, Ministry of Education, Government of Saint Lucia, 2001, www.saintluciancreole.dbfrank.net/dictionary/KweyolDictionary.pdf. Accessed 31 Jan. 2016.